The Night Before the ToothFairy

Grosset & Dunlap

To my dentist, Dr. Harry Johnson,
and his smiley staff.
—N.W.

For my two grandmothers, June and Lucille—
my own loving tooth fairies for so many years.
—J.N.

Library of Congress Cataloging-in-Publication Data is available.

ISBN 978-0-448-43252-6

The Night Before the ToothFairy

by Natasha Wing

Illustrated by Johansen Newman

Grosset & Dunlap • New York

'Twas the night before the Tooth Fairy
would come take my tooth.
I'd been so excited
ever since it got looth.

My bottom tooth was dangling
and twisting about.
Tonight was the night.
It just had to come out.

I wiggled it and waggled it
for such a long while.

My baby brother flashed me
his funny toothless smile.

Mom handed me an apple.
She said, "Here, take a bite."
"No! 'Cause if I swallow it,
guess who won't come tonight."

Dad said, "Let's yank it out
with a doorknob and string."
"No way, no how!" I told him.
"You're not gonna do a thing."

Then my brother grabbed our kitten
which scared our cockerpoo

who knocked me right over—
and out my tooth flew!

My brother looked around the floor
on his hands and his knees.

When he found it—
picture time!
We smiled and I yelled,
"Cheese!"

Then I ran to the mirror
and what did I see?
A cool gap in my smile,
where my tooth used to be.

I could stick a straw through it
then sip up my drink!

Or pretend I'm a fountain
and spray water in the sink!

"All righty," said Mom.
"Time to climb into bed,
or the Tooth Fairy may visit
some other house instead."

My tooth was put under
my pillow with care,
in hope that the Tooth Fairy
soon would be there.

I hopped in and nestled
all snug in my bed,
while visions of Fairyland
danced in my head.

When what to my wondering eyes
should appear,
but a twinkling glow—

the Tooth Fairy was here!

Her wand, how it glittered!
Her dimples, how merry!
Her wings were so sparkly,
so light and so airy!

She reached under my pillow—
I pretended to be sleeping—

and slipped my tooth
in a pouch
where it stayed for
safekeeping.

I kept one eye open,
as she fluttered around.

Then—poof!—she was gone
without making a sound.

I dug under my pillow
and felt something funny.

All right! The Tooth Fairy
left me some money!

"Look what I got!" I yelled
with a whoop and a holler.
"The Tooth Fairy gave me
a spanking new dollar!"

That woke up my brother
who started to cry.

When Dad picked him up,
we could see why.

Now my brother and I both have a new grin.
My first tooth came out—his first tooth came in!